spot

MIGHTY MACHINES

CONCRETE MIXERS

by Mari Schuh

AMICUS | AMICUS INK

chute

drum

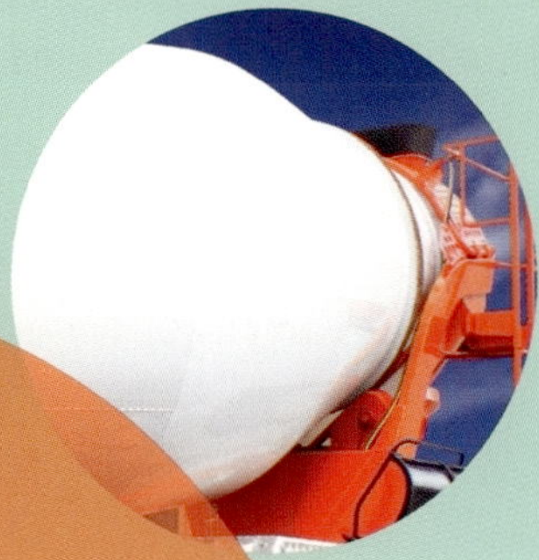

Look for these words and pictures as you read.

hopper

tank

Look! Here comes a concrete mixer! What can it do?

It mixes wet concrete.
Concrete is thick.
It is heavy.
Mix it up!

hopper

See the hopper?
It has a big hole.
Concrete is poured
in the hopper.
Down it goes!

drum

See the drum?
It is big. It spins.
It mixes the concrete.

See the chute? It is long.
The concrete flows down.
See it go!

chute

tank

See the tank?
It holds water.
Water cleans the drum.

A concrete mixer is busy.
It makes roads.
It makes walls too.
See it work!

chute

drum

Did you find?

hopper

tank

Spot is published by Amicus and Amicus Ink
P.O. Box 1329, Mankato, MN 56002
www.amicuspublishing.us

Library of Congress Cataloging-in-Publication Data
Names: Schuh, Mari C., 1975- author.
Title: Concrete mixers / by Mari Schuh.
Description: Mankato, Minnesota : Amicus, [2018] | Series: Spot. Mighty machines | Audience: K to grade 3.
Identifiers: LCCN 2016044425 (print) | LCCN 2016049256 (ebook) | ISBN 9781681510989 (library binding) | ISBN 9781681522098 (pbk.) | ISBN 9781681511887 (e-book)
Subjects: LCSH: Concrete mixers—Juvenile literature.
Classification: LCC TA439 .S357 2018 (print) | LCC TA439 (ebook) | DDC 629.225—dc23
LC record available at https://lccn.loc.gov/2016044425

Printed in the United States of America

HC 10 9 8 7 6 5 4 3 2 1
PB 10 9 8 7 6 5 4 3 2 1

To Jadyn —MS

Wendy Dieker, editor
Deb Miner, series designer
Aubrey Harper, book designer
Holly Young, photo researcher

Photos by Dreamstime 8–9; iStock cover, 1, 3, 4–5, 6–7, 12–13, 14–15; Shutterstock 10–11